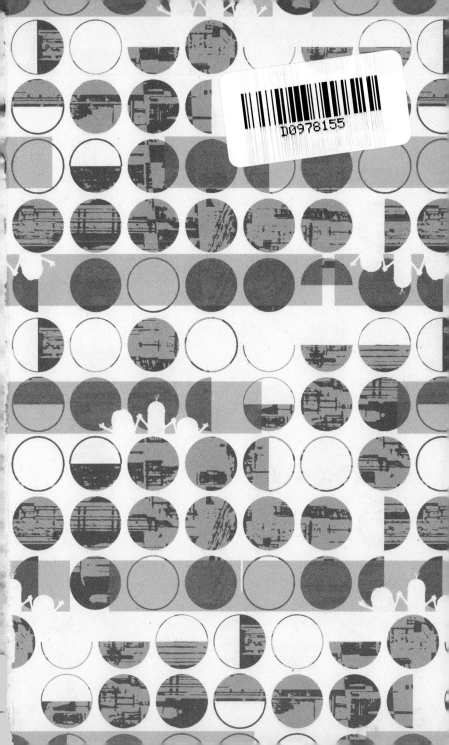
D0978155

MINIONS ™

MINIONS: THE JUNIOR NOVEL

A CENTUM BOOK 9781910114278

Published in Great Britain by Centum Books Ltd

This edition published 2015

2015 © Universal Studios Licensing LLC.

1 3 5 7 9 10 8 6 4 2

Minions is a trademark and copyright of Universal Studios. Licensed by

Universal Studios Licensing LLC. All rights reserved.

All rights reserved. No part of this publication may be reproduced,

stored in a retrieval system, or transmitted in any form or by any means,

electronic, mechanical, photocopying, recording or otherwise, without

the prior permission of the publishers.

Centum Books Ltd, Unit 1, Upside Station Building, Solsbro Road,

Torquay, Devon, UK, TQ2 6FD books@centumbooksltd.co.uk

CENTUM BOOKS Limited Reg. No. 07641486

A CIP catalogue record for this book is available from the British Library

Printed in Poland

The Junior Novel

Adapted by Sadie Chesterfield
Based on the Motion Picture Screenplay
Written by Brian Lynch

Prologue

Minions have been on this earth

since the beginning of time. At first, they were just shapeless, single-celled organisms searching for the biggest, baddest villain to serve. They'd follow anyone despicable enough—as they needed to be led by something bigger than themselves.

Over hundreds of years, the Minions evolved, growing arms and legs. As they evolved, so did their choice of leader. Each master was eventually replaced—or eaten—by a bigger, badder master. At one point, they followed the biggest amoeba—

until he was devoured by an evil fish who, in turn, was eaten by an evil amphibian. They followed that evil lizard right out of the prehistoric sludge and onto a beach...

...where he was smashed by a Tyrannosaurus rex.

The Minions were very impressed. They stared in awe at the giant T. rex, with his terrible claws and teeth. He was the greatest monster they had ever seen—so much bigger and tougher than their other master. It was love at first sight.

After that, they served the T. rex, scratching his scaly back and picking the bugs out of his nostrils. They spent days riding on him through the wilderness, helping him look for prey. They spent nights cleaning the mud and dirt from between his toes. But all good things must come to an end. The Minions had found a master, but it was not always easy to keep one.

One day, two Minions were trying to pull a banana from a bush (after all, Minions *love* bananas). The banana loosened a great big boulder, which started rolling down the side of a hill. The T. rex had been minding his own business when he saw the boulder rolling straight toward him. So he ran. The boulder picked up speed, overtaking the great dinosaur. The T. rex ended up on top of the boulder, running and trying to keep his balance. Unfortunately, he wasn't paying attention to where the boulder was headed.

The giant rock—with the T. rex running on top—rolled down the hill and stopped at the edge of a massive cliff. The dinosaur and the boulder teetered at the edge, overlooking the heated furnace of a bubbling volcano. The Minions ran to the top of the hill to make sure their master was okay. But two Minions bumped into each other, rolling toward the T. rex. One Minion hit the rock and stopped, but the second Minion kept tumbling closer and closer. The T. rex was delicately balancing on the boulder, and when the Minion stopped rolling just under the edge of the boulder, he took a deep sigh of relief. *Phew*. Close call.

That is, until the Minion picked himself up and bumped his head on the boulder—giving it that extra little tiny push, which caused the boulder and the dinosaur to tumble all the way into the volcano. *Whoops*.

The Minions stood there, looking over the edge into the hot lava, and cried, mourning the loss of the great T. rex.

Time to find a new master.

The Minions wandered the earth, looking for a new master. With the emergence of the Stone Age came the rise of a new species: mankind. The Minions took an instant liking to man and helped him as best they could as he battled the wild animals of the plains. When a bear came after him, showing its razor-sharp teeth and ready to strike, they handed the man a flyswatter.

It seemed like a good idea at the time.

It wasn't.

The bear made off with the caveman, leaving the Minions without a leader. The Minions mourned their master. For a while, they wandered the plains, sad and lonely. They were lost without someone to follow.

Many years later, they found another master worthy of their love and affection. A pharaoh in ancient Egypt used the Minions to build his pyramid. There was only one problem...the Minions built it upside down. Within minutes of finishing the triangular-shaped pyramid, it fell over, squashing their master flat.

But Minions do not give up. They do not know the meaning of the word "defeat" (mainly because they don't know a lot of words). They persist no matter what.

They found another master in the Dark Ages: a man who called himself Dracula, who had pale skin and terrible fangs. He kind of reminded them of the T. rex. They liked that.

Moving into Dracula's castle, they worked

hard to earn his trust. They cleaned cobwebs and crypts. They polished candlesticks and put in fresh new candles. And at the end of each day, they helped Dracula into his coffin, hung up his cape, and fluffed his pillow—but only after they reminded him to brush his fangs before bed. Over time, Dracula came to rely on the little yellow helpers and to think of them as his friends.

"Tomorrow vill be my three-hundred-und-fifty-seventh birthday," he told them. The Minions' heads swam with ideas of throwing the perfect birthday celebration. They made punch; they made cake; they even created the perfect present—a portrait of Dracula and all his Minions by his side.

"Surprise!" the Minions yelled.

"Aw, how vonderful." Dracula smiled, sipping from his goblet of blood punch.

"Big boss, big cake," said the Minions, revealing a giant cake with 357 candles on it. Then it was time for the gift. But it was too dark. How would their master be able to see all their hard work? So the Minions grabbed the thick, heavy curtains and gave them a tug. Bright, intense rays of sunlight poured into the room.

"Paratu, big boss," the Minions cooed, admiring their work of art.

Dracula didn't say anything. He didn't even move.

"Big boss?" they said.

Who knew that sunlight could turn Dracula to ash? Apparently, the Minions didn't. Dracula should have warned them about that. Really.

The Minions had bad luck with other masters, too. They almost killed Napoleon with a poorly aimed cannon blast. He was a little man, not much taller than the Minions, but he had a very big temper. He did not take their mistake lightly. His army pursued the Minions for hundreds of miles, deep into the snowy tundra. They finally found refuge in a cave hidden in a snowy mountain range.

The Minions spent weeks and then years there, forging their own civilization. At first it was fun.

They built snow-houses, had snowball fights, and ate snow cones. But something was missing. With no leader to serve, the Minions became aimless and depressed.

Decades passed, and the Minion village fell into a bottomless sadness. They didn't enjoy making snow cones anymore. They no longer climbed one another, building Minion towers, or played in the snow. Their games of Ping-Pong were abysmal. If they didn't find a master, and soon, the Minions would perish.

But all was not lost. For one Minion had hope. And he had a plan.

His name…

…was Kevin.

Chapter One

Kevin had kept quiet for some time, but he could not hold back any longer. He stepped forward in front of his tribe, preparing to reveal his big plan. He was going to leave the cave. He'd go out into the world and find the biggest, baddest villain to serve and then all his Minion friends could have purpose again. There was only one problem though...he needed help.

"Kiday come me?" he said, standing in front of the other Minions.

One of the tiniest Minions, Bob, raised his

hand. He jumped up and down, excited. "Me coming!" Bob yelled.

Kevin looked down at the little runt of a Minion. He was half Kevin's size. Kevin needed volunteers but was worried Bob wasn't strong enough for the dangerous journey ahead. "Uh… no. Una otra Minion?" Kevin asked.

But Bob kept waving his little arms in Kevin's face. "Me! Me! Chosa me!"

Thankfully, a Minion in the back raised a ukulele in the air. The crowd parted, revealing a sleepy one-eyed Minion whose friends were holding up the ukulele, playing a trick on him. The musical instrument belonged to him.

Stuart stood up, groggily, waving to the crowd. Everyone was clapping for him. "Me? Thank you, heh, thank you…," he said, not really sure why everyone was looking at him. He grabbed his ukulele and started playing it, with no clue he had just agreed to leave the cave with Kevin to search mountains and deserts for an evil master who might possibly kill them, if the lack of water and food didn't kill them first.

Maybe it was better he didn't know?

Kevin pushed him out of the spotlight and stepped forward. "Una otra?" he asked, scanning the rest of the crowd.

Bob was still jumping up and down in front of everyone. Then Bob grabbed a block of ice and held it over his own head to show how strong he was. His thin arms shook under its weight. "Kevin! Kevin!" he pleaded until it forced him down into the snow.

Still, he managed to peer out from underneath it, a bit dazed. "Chosa me, Kevin!"

Kevin looked over him at the other Minions, hoping another one of them would raise their hands. No one did. He stared down at Bob, pinned beneath the ice. Kevin knew Bob was his only other option. He'd need at least two Minions with him.

"Ugh...," Kevin huffed. "Komay."

Bob clapped his hands, excited. He grabbed his teddy bear, Tim, and was ready to go. The giant mass of Minions parted. "Big boss! Big boss!" they chanted as Kevin, Stuart, and Bob walked through them toward the cave exit.

They turned around one last time to look at their friends, wondering how long it would be before they saw them again.

"Kumbaya," Kevin, Stuart, and Bob cried out, rallying the other Minions. As Kevin set off first, his chest swelled with pride. They would find another master...they would return...or they would die trying.

Kevin felt pride. He was going to be the one to save his tribe. Stuart felt hungry, mostly. He was going to be the one to eat the banana he brought along for the trip. And Bob was frightened of the journey ahead. Kevin reassured him, telling him not to be afraid. "Okay," Bob said. "La kita le big boss!" And they were off to find their new boss!

The journey was treacherous. They hiked over the snowy mountains and down through the dense forests. When Bob grew tired, Kevin carried him on his head. They made their way down into the valley where the grass grew high.

Finally, after weeks of travel, they reached the ocean. Kevin and Stuart made a canoe out of a downed tree trunk. After a few days on the beach collecting bananas for the back of the boat, they set sail on the ocean. They paddled for miles, using oars they'd made out of branches and leaves. They drifted with the currents. They slept. They got hungry, and they started looking at one another strangely.

After they ran out of food, Stuart became so famished he started seeing things. To Stuart's amazement, Kevin and Bob looked exactly like delicious bananas! He lunged at Kevin and started licking him. Bob joined in. But just then, they saw the most incredible sight. Far off in the distance was a beautiful woman. She stood tall, staring out at the Minions in their tiny boat. She was dressed in long, elegant robes.

And she was…green?!

As soon as he saw her, Bob jumped out of the canoe and swam toward shore.

"Bob! Stopa!" Kevin called, looking up at the Statue of Liberty.

Kevin and Stuart continued paddling after Bob. The boat eventually drifted toward a pier. They had reached New York City in all its glory. They climbed onto the pier and walked up the sidewalk. Everyone was wearing something— blue jeans and hats, dresses and jumpers in the fashion of 1968. The Minions' coats were too heavy and hot for the warm weather. If they were going to fit in, they needed to look the part.

Luckily, the trio stumbled upon an alleyway between two buildings with clotheslines stretched across it. There were so many clothes to choose from. The Minions quickly climbed a fire escape to find some new apparel. First Stuart pulled down a colorful, tie-dyed shirt, but it was too big. Then he grabbed a pair of boxers, but they hiked up over his mouth. Kevin shook his head in disapproval. It was *not* a good look.

Finally, Kevin looked up and saw what he wanted gleaming in the sunlight above: overalls. Those would be perfect.

The three denim overalls looked like they were for little kids. The Minions pulled them on, replacing their dirty old coats from the cave, and admired their new looks.

"Bueno!" Stuart said, turning around so he could see his reflection in the glass window. His butt looked good...*real* good.

Then they took off through the streets, dwarfed by the giant buildings. Dwarfed by the hot-dog carts and the fire hydrants.

Dwarfed by everything, really.

As they made their way into Times Square, everything was new and shiny...and very, very big. A billboard high above had a picture of a man who was running for president—some guy named Nixon.

The Minions scrambled away. Maybe they were a little too eager to find a master. After hundreds of years of searching, they could afford to be a little more discerning now. They scanned the street, unsure which way to go. They pushed through a crowd of hippies protesting a war. They held signs that said PEACE and LOVE.

"War! What is it good for?!" a girl with flowers in her hair yelled.

"Boo-yah! Boo-yah!" Bob and Stuart joined in, raising their fists in the air.

Kevin had to drag them away. For a long while, they stood on the sidewalk, staring into the front of a music store. Stuart admired some awesome electric guitars in the shop window. He imagined himself in the photos of the famous rock legends. Then Bob got distracted by a woman in a banana-print dress. He followed her

out of the store and into a nearby taxi, which sped off. Stuart and Kevin searched for their friend, afraid they'd lost him forever. Finally, they spotted him going into a department store.

"Women's bell-bottoms and tie-dyed shirts are marked down!" a voice from the loudspeaker said as the two Minions ran around the store, looking for Bob. "Check out our wide selection of go-go boots and miniskirts."

They searched the whole store and finally found him in the dressing room. He was staring at the hundreds of Minions reflected in the mirror, as if they were his own tribe. Bob missed his friends, but Kevin reminded him of their important mission and Bob felt a little better. Then, suddenly, the lights went dark. The Minions wandered out of the dressing rooms to find that the entire store was deserted. The exits were locked. They'd be stuck inside for the entire night.

They tried to get comfortable. Kevin found a

big bed with a TV in front of it. It was so much nicer than the hard floor of the Minion cave. They all huddled together under the soft blankets and flipped on a TV show called *The Dating Game*. On the show, a man named Bob stood under a sign that said BACHELOR #1. He was short with a round belly.

"Yeah, go, Bob!" Bob cheered.

"Kevin?" the host asked. Another man stepped forward—bachelor number two. He was tall and lanky, and had a stiff, uptight vibe. He kind of looked like Minion Kevin…only taller.

"La Kevin!" Kevin cried. "C'est la me!"

"Or will it be Stuart?" the host added. A small, laid-back man with hair covering one eye was revealed.

"Yo, Stuart!" Stuart yelled.

As the bachelorette was about to decide who she'd go on her date with, the TV screen went to static. Stuart tried to fix the antennae, but it was no use. He stood on top of the TV, moving the two bunny ears back and forth, until suddenly another screen appeared....

VNC: VILLIAN NETWORK CHANNEL, it said.

A man in a black suit appeared on the screen. "You're watching the top secret Villain Network Channel," the broadcaster said, staring out at the audience. "If you tell anyone, we'll find you."

Kevin smiled, liking how evil this guy seemed. Not even one minute had passed and he was already threatening the audience.

Pictures flashed across the screen. There were shots of a giant convention with different villains. A young girl in a black cat costume. A giant ogre with a wooden club. Two mad scientists with test tubes that poured out red smoke. He'd never seen so many bad guys in one place.

"VNC is sponsored by Villain-Con. For eighty-nine years straight, the biggest gathering of criminals anywhere," the man said.

The Minions all leaned forward, listening to every word out of the man's mouth.

"C'est la! C'est la finte la big boss!" Kevin cried.

"Attend guest lectures from esteemed villains!" the man went on. "Make contacts in the underworld community. And, for the first time anywhere, a special appearance from the first female super villain…Scarlet Overkill!"

A woman's silhouette appeared onscreen, stealing from other criminals. Even her shadow seemed menacing. She looked at the camera as she defeated a group of mobsters. "Evil," the man said.

"So evil," Scarlet said.

"Criminal genius," the broadcaster said.

"Hey, a girl's gotta make a living," Scarlet said.

"Move aside, men! There's a new bad man in town," the broadcaster said. "And that man…is a woman!"

Scarlet stood on a pile of defeated villains and laughed.

"Crime isn't pretty," the broadcaster said.

Then Scarlet added, "It's red hot."

The Minions hadn't felt this happy in years. It was the same swell of joy they experienced when they saw the T. rex for the first time. They'd known it when they fought alongside Napoleon and slept in coffin beds beside Dracula.

This was it…the villain they'd been looking for. Their great and terrible master.

"Get to Villain-Con this weekend. Only at 545 Orange Grove Avenue in Orlando, Florida. So much fun, it's a crime," the man said.

Kevin stood up, jumping on the bed. "Villain-Con! Orlando! La big boss!"

Chapter Two

The next morning, Kevin, Stuart, and Bob stood at the side of the road. A bus drove past, spitting exhaust onto them. Kevin wiped the grime from his face.

They'd been waiting there for almost an hour, hoping they could get a ride to Orlando, wherever that was. Kevin stared at a man with a long beard and ripped jeans who was standing across the street. He stuck his thumb out, and a van stopped and picked him up. "Oh yeah, far-out, brother," he said as he climbed in.

Kevin picked up a piece of cardboard and

wrote ORLANDO on it in sloppy letters. Then he stuck his thumb out the same way the hippie had. It wasn't long before a station wagon came barreling down the road, speeding toward Kevin. It screeched to a stop inches from hitting him. The door opened, the dust parting to reveal an intimidating-looking couple in the front seat.

The man was wearing sunglasses and black gloves. The woman had a round face and a large head of golden curls, except for her perfectly cut bangs. She carved an apple with a knife. "Oh, Walter, look…," she said in a surprisingly happy voice. "These adorable little freaks are headed to Orlando, too."

"Yeah, I see that, Madge," Walter, the father, said. "Walter Jr.!"

Walter Jr. was the boy in the backseat. He rolled down his window. He stared at the Minions, his eyes small and beady. "What's happenin'?" he asked. He was so huge he took up half the car.

"Tina!" the father yelled.

Beside him, an excitable tween girl named Tina waved hello. She pushed the door open.

"All aboard the Nelson Express!" Walter bellowed. The Minions climbed in, with Kevin and Stuart in the backseat and Bob sitting in the front. Stuart was so close to Walter Jr. he could smell his armpits.

"Glad we came along before some weirdos picked you up!" Madge said. "Who wants apple slices?"

"Ooooh! Ooooooh! Bapple!" Bob cried.

Bob took one. Stuart offered his apple slice to Walter Jr. Walter Jr. stuck it in his mouth and swallowed it with one bite. Then he grabbed Stuart and gave him a noogie. "Thanks, man!" he said.

They hadn't been driving for more than an hour when Walter pulled the car over.

"Who needs to stretch their legs?" he asked.

Walter grabbed a ski mask from the glove compartment and pulled a gun out of the back of his pants. Tina and Walter Jr. pulled on their own ski masks. Even the family cat and Binky, the baby, put on ski masks.

"You guys wait here," Madge said. "We'll be right back."

The Minions turned, noticing the car was parked right outside a bank. All four of the Nelsons darted inside. An alarm sounded. There were screams and yells, and soon the Nelsons were running out with bags filled with cash. Dollar bills flew every which way behind them.

Tina and Walter Jr. squeezed into the backseat. Madge slammed the door shut behind her, nearly sitting on the cat. Walter climbed into the front seat and hit the gas, sending the car speeding down the street. "Okeydoke!" he yelled, pulling off his ski mask with one hand. "On the road again."

But just then, the Minions heard something strange—a far-off sound in the distance. They climbed up onto Walter Jr.'s shoulders, peering out the back windshield at the road behind them. Three cop cars had just rounded the corner. Their lights were flashing. Their sirens grew louder as they caught up with the Nelsons' car.

"Dad, we've got company!" Tina cried. "It's because I tripped the alarm. I stink!"

"Hey, we all make mistakes, sugarplum. You're still learning," Walter said, picking up speed. He pulled a brightly colored paint blaster out from under the front seat. Then he turned and leaned out the window, firing paintballs at the cop cars behind them. He covered two of their windshields with thick pink and orange paint. The cars screeched and skidded, nearly flipping over.

Meanwhile, Madge helped him reload from the passenger seat and gave Tina a pep talk.

"Your father's right. He wasn't this good at being evil overnight. Your time is coming!"

Only one car managed to keep up. The cop was going so fast he pulled right beside the station wagon. He glared at them through his passenger window.

"Pull over—now!" the cop yelled.

Walter fired again, but the paintball gun jammed. The police car slowed, then rammed into the back of the station wagon, knocking it off course. The Nelsons' car spun around, everyone flying to one side of it. When Walter finally straightened it out, he smiled. "Quick getaway, coming right up!" he yelled.

The criminal father shifted the car into reverse. The station wagon went screeching down the street backward, speeding away from the police officer. Kevin grabbed a tiny pistol. Stuart grabbed a huge missile launcher, which Kevin immediately tried to take for himself. As they fought over the weapons, Kevin kept grabbing at Stuart's launcher. Stuart accidentally fired the launcher at a telephone pole. The pole fell over, blocking the police car's path.

Within a few minutes, they'd completely lost them. "That was great!" Walter cried as he checked the rearview mirror one last time to make sure the coast was clear.

Madge glanced at the tiny Minions sitting between her kids. "Say, fellas…can we get personal for a second? Why are you headed to Orlando?"

The Minions were quiet. The man on the Villain Network Channel had been clear: The first rule of Villain-Con was to not talk about Villain-Con. They weren't supposed to tell anyone they were going there.

"Come on, you can tell us," Walter said. "You're going to Villain-Con, aren't you?"

Stuart smiled sheepishly. Was it that obvious?

"Villain-Con!" Bob sang out, unable to keep the secret any longer.

Walter smacked his hand on the steering wheel and laughed. "I knew it! I knew you were villains, didn't I, honey? What a small world! Hope we're not in rival gangs!"

Tina pulled a magazine out of the pocket in the seat in front of her. She flipped through the pages, showing it to Kevin. "When we get to Orlando, I'm gonna get all my favorite villains to sign my magazine. Dumo the Sumo, Frankie Fish-Lips, and, ohhhhh, my favorite—"

Kevin leaned in as Tina opened the center-fold. There was Scarlet Overkill, a stunning woman wearing all red. She held a crossbow as she stood on a pile of other villains. Kevin wiped his goggles. She had one of the meanest expressions he'd ever seen, her eyes narrowed as if she were shooting laser beams out of them.

"Scarlet Overkill, the coolest super villain, like, EVER!" Tina went on. "She started out as your average little girl—braces, pigtails. But by the time she was thirteen, she'd built a criminal empire. She's proof that you can commit any crime as long as you believe in yourself."

Kevin leaned down, his goggles just inches from the page. He'd never seen a more magnificent villain in all his life. She was better than the T. rex, better than any pharaoh or warrior that had come before her. He knew it then—he was certain.

"Scarlet le big boss!" he cried.

Chapter Three

Kevin and Bob had all fallen asleep. Stuart was wedged between Tina and giant Walter Jr., his face squashed into Walter Jr.'s armpit desperately trying to avoid a swinging tendril of spit dripping from Walter Jr.'s mouth. They hardly noticed when Tina sat up. She rolled down the window and pointed outside.

"We're here!" she yelled. The Nelson station wagon passed through desolate swamplands filled with alligators. There was nothing around for miles except a billboard that read, in big letters, ORLANDO! COMING SOON!

Walter drove the station wagon over the bumpy road until they finally stopped at a little wooden shack. Painted above the door were the words BAIT SHOP. Walter pulled the wagon up to a tiny microphone stand beside a sign that listed all the different kinds of bait. There were tiny critters and fish. MEALWORMS! $2 PER POUND! was written in sloppy handwriting.

"Welcome to Billy Bob's Bait Shop," a creepy voice said through the speaker. "How can I help you?"

Walter leaned out the window. "Hi, we're here for, uh…so much fun, it's a crime."

A bell on the speaker box rang. Without warning, the shack split open right in front of them. A giant metal tube snaked out of the ground and slammed over the station wagon, locking them inside. Then the tube lifted up again. It pulled the station wagon down into the ground, the shack closing shut around it.

Seconds later, the wagon landed hard on a metal platform. The Minions looked out the windows, realizing they were on a long conveyor belt moving into the underground convention hall. Bob jumped up and down. Kevin clapped his hands together.

"Villain-Con!" Stuart cried with excitement. "La Villain-Con!"

The conveyor belt let them off in a parking lot, where the station wagon came to a stop. They started walking toward the hall in a sea of villains of all shapes and sizes.

"Here we go! This is it!" Walter said, looking down at the three Minions. "I want to tell you, and I really—I really mean this—I really appreciate what you did back there with the cops. Really."

"Dad! It's Frankie Fish-Lips!" Tina said, shaking him. "I can smell him from here!"

Walter perked up. "Junior, get my camera!" he said excitedly. They ran toward the convention entrance.

"Good luck in there, boys," Madge said. "I hope you find what you're looking for!"

And within seconds the Nelsons were gone.

Stuart looked up at the convention center entrance. A banner above the doors read WELCOME TO VILLAIN-CON. "Yupaki mala Villain-Con!" Stuart yelled.

"Yeah!" Kevin and Bob cheered. "Villain-Con!"

They ran toward the main doors. When they got inside, there were villains everywhere they turned. Furry monsters roamed in packs. A thin evil scientist wandered past, a black cat in his arms. Tables displayed every kind of weapon the Minions could imagine—futuristic stun guns, metal crossbows, freeze guns, and poisonous darts.

Kevin, Stuart, and Bob kept going, taking in all the sights. A henchmen specialist was interviewing a fire-breathing lizard, trying to find him the right boss. Two mob bosses discussed their latest plot over drinks at the Parole Room Bar. Then, off in the distance, Kevin finally spotted her. A towering golden statue with the likeness of a beautiful and evil woman stood in the middle of the floor. It was Scarlet Overkill, their next potential Big Boss.

"Scarlet! Scarlet Popapeil!" Kevin yelled. He dragged Stuart and Bob behind him toward the hall where Scarlet was scheduled to appear. As the trio rushed through the convention, they noticed all the different booths that filled the floor. There was a booth for cracking safes. There was one for Freeze Rays. There was one for poisons and another for rockets. There was even a Professor Flux booth with several scientists that looked exactly the same. But the Minions didn't have time to stop and explore. They were in a hurry.

"Villain-Con presents our keynote speaker," a voice announced, "Scarlet Overkill: the world's first female super villain!" The announcer went on, urging everyone farther into the convention hall where Scarlet was speaking in just a few minutes.

"Stuart! Bob!" Kevin yelled, pulling them

through the crowd. "Ma puta la Scarlet Popapiel! Komay! Komay!"

When they got to the main hall, it looked like a giant rock concert was about to start. All the villains were crammed together, shoulder to shoulder, waiting for Scarlet to appear. Kevin, Stuart, and Bob stood on one another's shoulders, trying to get as good a view as possible.

This was the moment they'd been waiting for. All those days climbing snowy mountains and trekking through the thick grass to the beach… all those hours they spent trapped inside the Nelsons' car, breathing in Walter Jr.'s farts…this was what it was for. They were finally here: Villain-Con.

And they were about to meet their new master.

A silhouette of a woman appeared behind a large screen. Her voice sounded throughout the room. "Doesn't it feel so good to be bad?" Then, with one flourish, she burst through the screen, revealing Scarlet Overkill in all her glory. She was using her jet-pack dress to rocket above the ground. She stared out at the crowd. For just one moment, Kevin felt like she looked directly at him.

Everyone in the hall erupted in cheers. The clapping was so loud it hurt the Minions' eardrums. They didn't care, though. Kevin, Stuart, and Bob were in awe. They'd never seen such an amazing sight.

Chapter Four

"Scarlet! Scarlet! Scarlet!" the
crowd chanted.

Scarlet landed on the stage as her red jet-dress
retracted, folding up into a regular dress. She
looked around, completely calm, as if she always
had thousands of villains cheering her name.
"Oh wow, thank you," she cooed. "Oh, thank
you so much."

The crowd roared even louder.

Devoted fans were everywhere. Some were
cheering; others were screaming, "I love you,
Scarlet!" There was even a male fan and his

whole family, each of them dressed in red halter dresses so they matched Scarlet's outfit.

Finally, Scarlet narrowed her eyes at the shouting crowd, "Okay, now *shhhhhhh.*"

Everyone fell silent.

"When I started out," she said, "people said a woman could never rob a bank as well as a man. Well, times change. Look at all those faces out there. We are all so different. But we have one thing in common."

A half-man, half-fish villain named Frankie Fish-Lips raised his webbed hand. "We were born with flippers?" No one responded. He looked around, embarrassed. "No? Just me?"

"No, Frankie Fish-Lips," Scarlet said, putting her hands on her hips. "What we have in common is that we all have big dreams. And we will do anything to make them come true. Have any of you ever dreamed of working for the greatest super villain of all time? Well, what if I told you that I am looking for new henchmen?"

The Minions felt like they were going to

explode. Kevin rubbed his ears, making sure he'd heard her right. Did she just say she needed new henchmen?!

"I truly believe somewhere out there is a villain with the potential to serve greatness. And it could be any of you!" Scarlet went on. "It's just a matter of proving you're good enough. You see this little trinket?"

She held out her hand, showing the crowd a sparkling ruby. Everyone *ooh*ed and *aah*ed. "Just take it from my hand and you've got the job. No big deal. It's almost too simple…."

The Minions eagerly moved toward the stage, but hundreds of villains were in front of them, rushing there first.

"That job is mine!" a goon with slicked black hair cried. He climbed up over the edge of the stage, trying to get to Scarlet.

She leveled her eyes at the villain. "Oh, you've got something right…," she said, pointing to one of his nostrils. "There!"

She pulled her fist back, then pummeled him

in the nose. The goon went flying backward off the stage, his arms spinning in circles as he tried to keep his balance. He hit the floor with a horrible thud.

That didn't stop other villains from coming forward, trying to get the gem from Scarlet. A lumbering oaf with buckteeth lunged at her, but she spun around and kicked him in the side of the head, knocking him out cold. A man with a black cape and mask tried to rush the stage from behind. Scarlet saw him just seconds before he got to her. She turned and landed her elbow into his jaw.

"Oh, look at you!" she yelled, kicking another villain in the face.

Wham! She jumped in the air and hit a woman dressed as a spider in the ribs. "Love the costume!" She laughed.

Kevin looked at the pile of bodies on the edge of the stage, terrified. They came here to find the biggest, baddest boss they could, but they wanted to leave with their arms and legs intact. He grabbed Stuart and Bob, pulling them back into the crowd and toward the door.

They tried to move between the rest of the villains' legs, but the crowd kept pushing them forward. Hundreds of villains were still trying to get the gem from Scarlet, even as she fought them off, sending them flying into walls.

Bob stumbled, and Tim, his teddy bear, slipped from his hands. The worn bear was kicked across the stage by another villain. Bob darted around, trying to get him back.

"Who's next?" Scarlet yelled. She glanced around, waiting for someone else to come at her. "Is no one good enough?"

A villain with a huge sword charged her. She jumped back, kicking the blade out of his hand with both her heels. The sword fell on the stage with a *clack!* and she grabbed it, flinging it into the face of a villain wearing a kilt.

Three more villains came at her, and three more villains were thrown off the stage. At a certain point, the ruby slipped from her hands.

Kevin and Stuart could see it thrown high, then disappear somewhere behind Scarlet as she pummeled a woman who tried to breathe fire at her. Bob was lost in the pile of bodies. He was still climbing over the wounded, looking for his teddy bear, Tim.

When Scarlet had fought off the last of the villains, she looked around. Half the auditorium was empty now. A bunch of bad guys were sitting on the ground, still dazed from her punches.

"Ugh!" she yelled. "Didn't my speech inspire anyone to rise up and prove themselves worthy? All these villains and yet I still have the—"

Scarlet looked down at her hand, realizing for the first time that she didn't have the ruby anymore. Instead she was holding Bob's teddy bear. In the scuffle, she'd somehow grabbed it.

"Why do I have this bear?!" she yelled. "Wait! Who has the ruby?"

Bob sat on the edge of the stage and coughed, spitting the ruby onto the floor in front of her.

Scarlet rubbed her eyes, as if she couldn't believe what she was seeing. She looked from Bob to Kevin to Stuart. "Whoa…who are you, my knights in shining denim?"

Kevin climbed onto the stage. "Me le Kevin, la c'est Stuart"—he pointed to Stuart, then Bob—"et la le Bob."

"Minions!" Bob yelled, explaining and holding out a business card.

Scarlet smiled a wicked smile, her teeth sparkling. She threw her hands out to the side, introducing her new little friends. "Behold! The last creatures you'd expect to win the day have emerged victorious! The job has been filled! Everyone meet my new henchmen, the Minions!"

Kevin, Stuart, and Bob stood on the stage, looking out at what was left of the audience.

They held their hands together and raised them in the air, taking a bow. Kevin smoothed his few strands of hair, making sure he looked all right. He suddenly wished they'd washed their overalls before coming to Villain-Con. He wasn't expecting all this attention.

The Minions stared out at the crowd, spotting a familiar face. The Nelson family was standing in the first few rows. They cheered for the Minions.

"Hey! I know those guys!" Walter shouted at the Grim Reaper, who was standing right next to him. "I gave 'em a ride here!"

He was so excited he shook the Grim Reaper, accidentally causing him to fall apart into a pile of bones.

When the Minions first emerged from the ocean, they knew one thing: They needed a despicable master!

During prehistoric times, the Tyrannosaurus rex was considered the king of the dinosaurs. Naturally, the Minions made him their king as well.

As time went on, the Minions moved from evil master to evil master. They had many, many masters. But they rarely lasted.

For a little while, they even worked for the master of vampires—Dracula himself. At least until one sunny birthday...

Who's a better evil master—a pirate or a shark?

The Minions even had a part in the French Revolution under the great—but rather small—Napoleon Bonaparte.

After centuries and centuries of losing their masters, the Minions retreated to ice caves in the Arctic. But in time, they grew sad.

That's when Kevin, Stuart, and Bob stepped up. They couldn't wait any longer—they decided to go find a new evil master!

Their journey led them to a most terrifying place—New York City! From there, they went south toward Florida.

At Villain-Con—
the world's foremost
gathering of
villains—they met
the queen of villainy:
Scarlet Overkill.

Scarlet had lots of evil plans in store for her Minions.

But when it comes to the Minions, plans don't always go according to plan. Long live King Bob!

Chapter Five

Within minutes, Scarlet had whisked them away from the auditorium. The Minions were down in the basement of the parking garage, climbing into Scarlet's sleek, futuristic red jet. She slipped on a pair of sunglasses and put her hand on the controller in the center console.

"Buckle up, boys...," she said, smiling. Kevin, Stuart, and Bob scrambled to get into the seats behind her. They pulled on their belts and grabbed the armrests, preparing for takeoff.

"Next stop: England!" Scarlet yelled. She

pressed a button on the controller, and the jet blasted out of the Villain-Con parking lot. They rocketed into the sky, high above Orlando, the marshes disappearing beneath them. Kevin used one of the phones in the back of the plane to call the Minions in the snow cave. He couldn't wait to tell them the big news: They'd found their new boss.

But when Kevin called his tribe, they told him they had already found a big boss: a group of yetis who had wandered over to the cave. While Kevin spoke to Dave on the phone, the other Minions sang and danced for the yetis, wanting to impress them with their entertainment skills. Between the choreographed dance routines, the theatrics, and, of course, the amazing Minion band, the yetis were more than happy. That is, until the tuba player blew too hard, causing the ice to crack on the ceiling. This loosened one large chunk of ice—which fell directly onto the head of the leader yeti, killing him.

"Uh, Kevin? Tu le dissay England?" Dave said

nervously as the yetis growled. The Minions were immediately chased out of the cave and back into the snowy wasteland.

"Bello? Bello? Que pasa?" Kevin asked as he listened to nothing but dial tone. He hung up, feeling worried for his friends.

The jet traveled so fast it wasn't long before they reached England. Scarlet's castle appeared on a majestic hill in the center of London. It was the biggest structure for miles, a towering thing with stone turrets and a giant wall around it.

Scarlet landed the jet effortlessly, touching down on the runway outside. She maneuvered the jet into a giant hangar. The Minions looked around, impressed by how big it was. It must've been ten times the size of their old cave.

The Minions followed Scarlet down a staircase on the far side. "Herb! My baby!" Scarlet called out.

"You know I am," Herb cooed. A portion of the ceiling lowered down, revealing a man sitting in an armchair. He wore a sleek pin-striped suit. The chair spun around so he was facing them. "How'd it go? Were you evil?"

"Soooo evil," Scarlet said softly. She turned to the Minions, who were still hovering by the staircase, watching the scene unfold. "Come, meet my husband, Herb. Inventor, super genius, fox. Herb, these are the new recruits: Kevin, Stuart, and Bob."

"Bello!" Kevin said, walking over. "Paratikota."

Herb looked down at the Minions, studying their overalls and goggles. "Right on." He laughed. "You guys are crazy little and way yellow, and I dig that. Come on...we'll show you around."

Scarlet and Herb led the Minions into a glass elevator on the other side of the lair. They went down several floors to the bottom of the castle, where the doors opened into Scarlet's trophy room. The place was packed with paintings, rare cars, and antiques Scarlet had stolen.

"Whoa! Coolos!" they cried.

"I know, right?" Scarlet said, waving at all kinds of rare and valuable things. "Just some things I stole to help fill the void."

Stuart stood staring at one corner of the room, where rock-and-roll memorabilia was heaped in a pile. There were old guitars and records, signed platinum albums, and a vest Janis Joplin had worn. He ran up to a painted guitar. "Whoa! La mega-ukulele!" he yelled.

"Stuart!" Scarlet yelled. "Don't touch the guitar!"

Stuart backed away slowly. Meanwhile, Bob was inspecting a painting of a Campbell's soup can by some guy named Andy Warhol.

"Checking out my can?" Herb asked. "We stole that because finally someone expressed my love of soup in painting form."

Scarlet spun around, facing the Minions. Her expression grew serious. "Okay, listen up! It's time to get down to business." She walked up to a painting of a woman with short, curly brown hair. She was wearing an evening gown and fur, and had a crown on her head. "Do you know who this is?"

"La cucaracha?" Kevin asked.

"This is Queen Elizabeth," Scarlet said. "Ruler of England. Oh…I love England. The music, the fashion; I'm seriously thinking of overthrowing it someday. Anyway, this pale drink of water oversees it all. I'm her biggest fan, love her work…and I really, really, really want her crown. Steal me the crown, and all your dreams come true. Respect! Power!"

"Banana!" Stuart cheered.

"Banana!" Scarlet repeated enthusiastically, if not a little confused. But first—they needed to get outfitted for the job at hand. Scarlet sent them to Herb's lab to get some gear.

Chapter Six

The Minions climbed down into

Herb's lab. There was a giant metal contraption in the corner, with mechanical arms sticking out of the top. They crept toward it, trying to see what it was.

"No!" Herb cried. He rappelled down from a platform above, using a grappling hook and rope. "Don't get too close, boys. When it's completed, it'll be my ultimate weapon, but right now it's leaking radiation like you would not believe."

The Minions stepped back, noticing the blue

puddle that oozed out the bottom of it. "So you're here for gear?" Herb asked.

The Minions nodded. Scarlet had told them to come here to get outfitted for the crown heist. Apparently, Herb had all the best henchman tools—fancy grappling hooks, stun guns, and fireproof suits.

Herb looked down at Bob. "Rob, Robert, Bobby. My boy! You get my far-out Stretch Suit—let me demonstrate."

Suddenly, Herb's arm stretched out. First just a few feet, then a few more, until it went out the window. Somewhere in the distance, they heard a woman scream. When he pulled his arm back, he had a chicken leg in his hand. "Mmm… chicken," Herb said, taking a bite. Herb removed the mechanical stretch arm with the chicken leg still in its grip and handed it to Bob. The Minion inspected it, smiling.

"Kevin," Herb went on. "Kev-bo. Seventh Kevin. You are the proud owner of my Lava-Lamp Gun. This baby shoots actual lava." Herb held up a gun, and a drop of red lava came out, burning a hole in the floor. He handed the gun to Kevin. It was so heavy Kevin could barely hold it.

"And finally, Stu," Herb said. "Stu-art. Stu-perman. Beef Stu. I got you the coolest invention, probably ever. Behold the Hypno-Hat!" Herb handed an orb-shaped helmet to Stuart. As soon as Stuart put it on his head, it began affecting Kevin and Bob. Bob's eyes rolled back, and he started clucking like a chicken.

"You can use it to hypnotize anyone. Anyone! But remember: With great power comes a great hat!" Herb added. "It's unbelievable, but you gotta believe it!"

Just then, Scarlet entered the lab. She strode over to Herb and wrapped her arms around him. "Oh, Herb," she cooed. "What Picasso is to paint, you are to illegal weapons and unlicensed, barely tested survival gear."

The Minions stood in front of their leader with their new stuff. Scarlet looked down at them, smiling at her new henchmen. She had never been more proud.

"It's getting late and you guys have had a big day. You must be exhausted. Let me show you to your room." She led them to a spare bedroom with massive decorations made out of axes and maces. Then she helped the Minions onto the big bed. Bob began to bounce up and down excitedly. "Boooing! Boooooing!" He laughed.

"Maybe I should settle you down with a little bedtime story. How does that sound, Bob?"

Bob stopped bouncing. He asked, "Bedtime porry?"

Scarlet sat on the edge of the bed. "Once upon a time, there was a magic land, far, far away from here…and in that magic land, there were three little pigs." She tapped each of the Minions on their head as she said it.

"One fateful day, the pigs encountered a big bad wolf…who had a wonderful surprise for them! The wolf offered the three piggies and all their friends a job working for her. Everyone would be so happy! It was everything they ever wanted! All the three little piggies had to do was steal ONE LITTLE CROWN that the beautiful wolf had wanted ever since she was a penniless little street kid. Unloved, abandoned. The thought of that crown was the only thing that made this little wolf happy. So she sent the pigs to get that crown."

Bob could almost see the story in his head. He imagined the three little Minions as pigs, following their leader around. Scarlet was the biggest, baddest wolf of all. They would travel around the world in her jet, stealing paintings and jewels. Then he imagined them stealing the queen's crown.

"But the little pigs were sloppy! They failed their mission!" Scarlet continued.

"So the wolf huffed and puffed...," Scarlet started. "And she blew them off the face of the earth!"

Bob could see it—how Scarlet would kill all three of them if they messed up. She'd squash them like little Minion bugs.

Her face was bright red. Her eyebrows were two harsh lines. She looked like she might burn holes in their head with her vicious stare.

"The end," Scarlet said with a smile. Suddenly, her expression returned to normal. She again patted the Minions on the head one by one. "Good luck getting that crown tomorrow, little piggies! I know you won't disappoint me."

Then she hopped off the bed and closed the door, leaving the piggies…errrr…*Minions* in darkness. Kevin and Stuart held each other tight, both extremely frightened by Scarlet's story. They looked over at Bob, hoping he would join them. But he was fast asleep with Tim, his teddy, clutched warmly in his arms.

Chapter Seven

The next morning, the Minions

headed out. They were off to the Tower of London to go steal the Queen's crown. The easiest way to get in was through the front door, but they needed tickets for that. So the three friends found an attendant and asked for tickets. The grumpy old woman shook her head, saying, "No children allowed unless accompanied by an adult." She shooed them away. What they needed was a disguise. So they snuck in by dressing themselves as a woman. Bob hopped onto Stuart's and Kevin's shoulders and put on a long dress to cover them. The look was completed by a huge red wig.

They took off the disguise as they searched the hallways. They soon found a door marked STRICTLY FORBIDDEN. They snuck inside and put on the gear Herb had given them, Bob pulling the Stretch Suit up over his tiny arms.

As they crept toward the crown jewels room, a group of guards approached. They all wore red jackets and tall, furry black hats with straps around their chins. "What are you doing here?" one of them called out, blocking the doorway.

"Pasteka?" Kevin asked nervously.

"This is a restricted area! Hands in the air!" another guard yelled.

Stuart pushed in front of his friends, moving closer to the guards. He hit the button on the side of his Hypno-Hat and began singing a song he'd heard on the radio in Scarlet's jet. The guards looked down at his helmet. Their eyes rolled back in their heads. At first, they tried to fight it, but soon they couldn't. They started dancing around and singing the song. They began to throw off their hats and jackets while they sang, revealing long, wild strands of hair, which they swung along to the beat.

The Minions knew this was their chance. They ran past the guards and up a long flight of stairs toward the back entrance of the crown jewels room. Scarlet had shown them an intricate map early that morning, which gave them a clear route to the inner rooms of the tower. Now that they'd gotten the guards out of the way, the only thing separating them from the crown was a giant steel door.

Kevin pulled out his Lava-Lamp Gun and aimed it at the center of the door. His hand trembled as he fired the first blast. The spot of lava melted a hole right through the steel. They waited a moment, letting it cool, before stepping inside.

There, at the end of the room, was the Queen's

crown. "Topilano la crowna!" Kevin cried, staring at the gleaming gold and jewels. "Comme!"

They ran toward it, only stopping when a man stepped out of the shadows. His face was covered with deep wrinkles. He had white hair and a cane. "So you came for the Queen's crown, did you?" he said. "Well, you're going to have to get through me. The Keeper of the Crown!"

He was pointing at the other side of the room with his cane, but Kevin realized the old man couldn't see. He wasn't even sure where they were. Kevin started laughing, but as soon as the man heard him, he leaned down, whacking Kevin over the head with the cane. He hit him again and again.

"I've been up here for decades, just waiting for someone to try to steal the Queen's treasure!" the old man yelled.

"Okay, me le do ay," Stuart said as he stepped forward. He aimed his helmet at the Keeper of the Crown. Then he brought his hand to the button on the side of it, about to hypnotize him, but the old man was too blind to see the hypnotic rays—it didn't work!

The crown's display case began to lower into the floor. Kevin pointed at it, upset. "Oh no! La crowna!" he yelled.

"What are you—yellow?" the Keeper yelled. "Come on, fight fair!"

Kevin aimed the Lava Gun at him, trying to keep the old man back. The man held out his rapier and blocked the end of the gun. When Kevin finally did shoot, the lava splattered all over the room, burning holes through the walls.

The Minions hopped onto the top of the crown case as it descended into the floor. They needed to get to the crown, but it was enclosed in a tube of glass and metal. Bob used his Stretch Suit arm like a can opener and started prying the top of the case off. Just then, the case stopped lowering and started sliding forward. The doors were about to open and expose them to all of London. Kevin, Stuart, and Bob hid just as the crown was taken by the queen's guards. Kevin, Stuart, and Bob followed, trying to catch up.

They ran through the courtyard outside the Tower of London. As they got to the exit, the guards were bringing the crown into a horse-drawn carriage. They ran and ran, as fast as their tiny legs could take them, but the carriage pulled away, taking the crown with it.

The Minions followed, but the horse-drawn carriage was moving too fast. It was impossible to keep up. Up ahead, there were thousands of people in the street. Everyone was smiling and waving at the woman in the front seat of the carriage. Kevin, Stuart, and Bob realized it was the queen herself. And more than likely, she was wearing the crown…which would make it that much harder to steal.

When they were just about to give up, Bob remembered his Stretch Suit. Bob made his legs two stories high. He grabbed his friends, one in each arm, and started running after the carriage, trying to catch up to the queen.

As they got close, they could see the queen waving at the people in the streets. But now, the royal guards were chasing after them. "Go for the legs!" one yelled as he watched Bob stretch over the crowd.

One of the guards wrapped his meaty arms around one of Bob's legs. Bob flung Kevin and Stuart into the carriage as he fell forward, losing his balance.

Kevin saw his opportunity. He pushed the driver out onto the sidewalk and grabbed the reins. The queen was behind him, screaming as the carriage bumped over the uneven street, the horses startled from all the commotion.

"Get back here!" another guard yelled. "The queen's been kidnapped!"

"What's going on?" the queen asked, looking around. Stuart settled into the seat beside her. He didn't answer. Instead, he flung himself at her head, trying to yank off the crown.

"Gimme la crowna!" he yelled. He put the queen in a headlock, then tried to wrestle the crown away. She broke free and punched him in the face.

"Gentlemen do not steal ladies' crowns!" she yelled.

By now, most of the police knew the queen's carriage had been hijacked by the Minions. Hundreds of them appeared from out of the crowd, chasing after the carriage as it headed for the River Thames. Bob broke free from one of the guards and chased after the carriage, too, hoping he could get to it before anyone else did. He used his super-stretch arms to pull it back just before it crashed into the river. But he only saved the queen and her crown for a brief moment. His arms acted like a rubber band, sending them all flying back toward the city.

The carriage was in the air. The queen and the Minions screamed as they headed toward a giant tree that stood in the center of the city square. It was coming closer…closer…They were flying right toward it….

Wham! They landed hard, the carriage breaking against the tree trunk. The queen, Kevin, and Stuart all spilled out, dazed.

Stuart struggled to get away from the crushed carriage. As soon as he broke free, he grabbed the crown from the queen's head. The queen yanked it back, holding it tight in her arms. "You scoundrel!" she cried. "After them!" she yelled to the police.

The Minions ran away from the police officers that were chasing them. Bob ran all the way toward a platform in the city square. A plaque beside it read THE SWORD IN THE STONE. He approached the platform and grabbed a sword that was wedged inside a giant boulder.

He clutched it tight, and the sword flew out. Then he turned to face the police. He was about to use it to fend them off, but the entire crowd was silent. The clouds above parted. A light shone down between them, casting Bob in a heavenly glow. A choir of young boys began singing a hymn.

It had long been said that no one except a true

king could pull the sword from the stone. Centuries had passed, and the sword had stayed there. But now, after so many years, Bob had done it. He was the king on high, the only worthy ruler of England.

The massive crowd dropped down to one knee, bowing before him.

Chapter Eight

A reporter stood outside Buckingham Palace, watching as Bob's limo pulled up the long driveway. "One of England's most famous myths has become a reality, as a new king has been crowned," he said, talking into the camera. "Bob, who appears to be a bald, jaundiced child, has pulled the famed sword right from its stone, which, legend dictates, makes him the new king."

At the lair, Scarlet was watching the broadcast. "Tiny yellow traitors!" she shouted, kicking over her TV. She angrily got into her Scarlet-Jet. She would teach those Minions to cross her.

Back at the palace, a line of guards stood by the palace entrance. Bob stepped out of his car, and the men all dropped to one knee. Per his request, they were all wearing neon-yellow outfits and blue overalls. They even had their own sets of black goggles.

"Awwwww, buddies!" Bob yelled, hugging each of the guards as he went past. "Buuuuddies!!!" They looked like all his friends from back in the cave. Even though he'd only been at the palace for a few minutes, it already felt like home.

Bob walked through the palace halls, Stuart and Kevin trailing behind him. They made their way up to one of the balconies that looked over the crowds below. The French doors were wide open. Bob could see the overcast sky. He could hear the cheers of the English people outside. They were waiting for him—their king, their master.

Bob approached the podium and took a deep breath, preparing to speak to his followers for the first time. He stared at the old couples with their canes and walkers, the families huddled together in heavy coats, and the young ones holding up signs for him. These were his followers now...his Minions. He met their gaze and said the deepest, most profound words that came into his head. "King Bob!!!"

"King Bob!!!" the crowd shouted back.

He went on to give a rousing speech. It was a shame no one understood a word of it. When he was finally done, the crowd stared back at him blankly. "King Bob!" Bob yelled again. The people cheered, applauding again.

The Minions enjoyed their freedom in the palace. They'd never had luxuries like this, no matter who their masters were. They had an unlimited supply of all the best foods—roasted duck and plump caviar. They could go anywhere and do anything—Bob slid down the polished wood railings. He raced Kevin and Stuart through the halls. (They liked to see how many expensive statues they could knock over. The one of Queen Victoria was their favorite.)

When they needed to go outside, they hopped on the palace corgis and went onto the lawn to play polo with the nobles. When they needed to be entertained, the palace guards put on a variety show, singing and dancing through the great hall. And when they just needed to relax, they hung out in the palace steam room.

That was always a little awkward.

Stuart liked to strut around in his neon thong.

Kevin and Stuart watched as Bob had his portrait painted. They played in the hall, tossing the polo ball back and forth between the palace advisor's legs. Kevin hit the ball across the room. Just then, the door swung open, and a familiar face appeared. The polo ball smacked Scarlet Overkill right in the nose.

"How dare you!" she yelled, her face red. One of the corgis jumped into her arms and licked her face, not knowing how furious she was.

"Scarlet!" Kevin cried, happy to see her.

"Don't you *Scarlet* me," she fumed. "You backstabbing little traitors! Using Herb's inventions to make yourselves king?"

Herb appeared in the doorway behind her. "I feel used," he said sadly. "I'm not going to lie…."

"You stole my dream!" Scarlet went on. "I was going to conquer England one day. There was going to be a coronation, and I was going to be made queen. Every moment was planned. I'd wear a dress so sparkly it glowed, and everyone who ever doubted me would be watching, and they would be crying. I was going to be the picture of elegance and class, and you pinheads screwed it up!"

Kevin plucked the crown from Bob's head and ran over to Scarlet, handing it to her. The truth was they liked living in the palace, but they had stolen the crown for her—everything else was an accident.

"La crowna!" Kevin cried. "Para tu."

The royal advisor held up his hands. He was a stern-looking fellow with a thick mustache. "No, no!" he yelled. "You cannot just abdicate the throne. And you definitely cannot just give the job to this woman. There are laws!"

"Laws?" Bob asked. "Maka te laws."

He pushed out the door, waving for the others to follow. He took the group all the way to Parliament, where the laws of England were made. If Scarlet wanted to be queen, she should be queen. After all, she was their master. Their fearsome leader. Their big boss.

Who was he to stand in her way?

Bob hopped over the wood bench in the middle of Parliament. He threw on a giant white wig that all the most official officials wore. Then he pounded the gavel on the table a few times.

"La keena pota Scarlet po papiel!" he shouted, declaring Scarlet the queen of England.

A reporter stood outside, watching the scene unfold. "King Bob has officially changed the law, clearing the way for Scarlet Overkill to be crowned Queen of England," he said, frowning into the camera. "She will be coronated at London's historic Westminster Abbey. If I wasn't so polite, I'd say this spells certain doom for the country, if not the world. But I'm so very polite, that I will keep my big mouth shut."

Then the reporter lowered his voice, inching closer to the camera so only the audience could hear.

"But seriously...," he whispered, "we're all in big trouble."

Just then, the broadcaster man from the VNC commercial hopped in front of the reporter. "Scarlet Overkill is the new Queen of England!" he said. "Criminals everywhere, come on down!"

Chapter Nine

As soon as they returned to the palace, Scarlet held a press conference. "I just want to thank the Minions for going above and beyond the call of duty," she said to the reporters. "You are three tiny, golden, pill-shaped miracle workers, and you have stolen not just England, but my heart."

She turned to the Minions. "Come with me," Scarlet said, leading them into the palace. Kevin took out his wallet and showed Scarlet the huge foldout section of pictures of his tribe. He asked, "Le buddies?"

Scarlet eyed it carefully and said, "Wow, so many of you! Well, you'll all get what you deserve."

The Minions skipped through the palace. This was it—finally their master would reward them for all their hard work. They had gotten her the crown, just like they promised, and she would be the Queen of England for years to come. Scarlet led them into the palace dining room, then through the kitchen, pointing to the stairwell at the far end, behind the refrigerator. Kevin, Stuart, and Bob had only taken a few steps down into the dark room when Scarlet slammed the door behind them.

Slowly, their eyes adjusted to the dark. The stone room smelled like mold. There were chains and whips hanging on every wall. Metal torture devices were covered with dust and cobwebs. There was even a giant metal bed with a razor-sharp blade above it.

She'd led them right into the palace dungeon....

Scarlet stared at them through the window in the door. She looked angry now, her face twisted with rage. "I don't want you to take this the wrong way, but I hate you," she sneered. "I thought I could get over what you did, but I feel so betrayed. I think, yes, I think we're going to have to break up. And it's not you...oh wait...hold on. It *is* you. It's one hundred percent you."

The Minions turned back to all the medieval machines. The dungeon master was already there, wearing a pin-striped suit and a hood to hide his face. Stuart was shaking so much he could barely talk. Bob pulled Tim, his teddy bear, close.

Scarlet looked at them one last time and smiled. "Get comfortable, Minions. Get real, real comfortable. Because this is where you're going to spend the rest of your worthless little lives."

With that, she was gone. Kevin, Stuart, and Bob all huddled together by the door, afraid to take even one step into the room. The man in the hood turned to them.

"All right, let's do this!" he said cheerfully. "Scarlet wants you tortured, so that's what we're going to do. We've got knives, and pokers—"

"Para tu?" Kevin asked, stepping forward. He looked at the man's eyes under the hood. He could have sworn his voice was familiar...he could've sworn it was Herb. "Moca la Herb!"

The man laughed. "Who's this handsome Herb fella? No, my name is...uh...*Blerb*. I'm a, uh, dungeon master. Prepare for torture...which I do!"

Within minutes, Blerb had them on the stretching rack, which pulled their hands and legs in opposite directions. The Minions stretched quite easily. In fact, it felt good.

Blerb tried another machine, but that didn't hurt the Minions, either. Instead, they broke free, swinging on the ropes in the dungeon, spinning up and around like they were circus performers.

Stuart did an impressive triple flip.

Kevin and Bob cheered.

"There's no laughing in the dungeon!" Blerb yelled. But even he was getting tired of this whole "torture" business. He couldn't stretch the Minions; he couldn't hang them up by their feet. Everything he did just made them laugh, like he was the most ridiculous dungeon master in the world. And it was kind of fun.

Soon they were all goofing around together, taking pictures of the medieval equipment with Blerb's Polaroid camera. Blerb made Kevin take a snapshot of him in the stockade, looking half dead. Then he took pictures of Kevin and Stuart playing with the giant axes on the wall. Blerb took a selfie that made it look like a spear was going straight through his head.

The four of them kept jumping around on the equipment, swinging from the whips and chains. Suddenly, a voice crackled over the castle inter-com. "Will the future king of England please come upstairs to prepare for the coronation?" Scarlet yelled.

Blerb straightened up. He stared down at the Minions, suddenly serious. "Well...I hope you learned your lesson for the day...."

Then he turned and left the dungeon. But he popped his head in the door one more time, lowering his voice so Scarlet couldn't hear. "And by the way...it was me, Herb, the whole time! I don't even know anyone named Blerb!"

The Minions laughed as Herb slipped out of the dungeon, the door falling shut behind him.

Chapter Ten

The Minions were trapped. They could hear things going on in the palace upstairs, but there was no way to get out, and the coronation would be starting shortly. They were looking around the dark, dank dungeon when Kevin noticed a sewer grate. That could be a way out. He and Stuart tried to pull the cover off, but it took some real effort. Finally, they opened it and crawled inside, Bob right behind them.

They walked in the dark until they found a ladder that led up into another building. They peered out from under the floorboards, realizing they were in the middle of a funeral home. People were wearing black and crying. A coffin was just a few feet away. They ducked back down into the sewer, but not before Bob grabbed a wreath of flowers. "Para la Scarlet!" he said, dragging it behind him. It was the perfect present for when Scarlet was officially crowned queen.

Kevin, Stuart, and Bob kept moving through the sewers. Along the way, Bob made friends with a pudgy little rat and decided to bring him along. With Tim in one arm and Poochie the rat dangling from the other, Bob followed Kevin and Stuart to the sewer exit near Westminster Abbey. It was the building where the coronation was taking place. They tried the front doors—they were already locked. Stuart rammed his head against the wood, but that didn't really work. At all.

They would have to climb the side of the building to get in. Kevin told Bob that it was time to say good-bye to Poochie, so Bob sang Poochie a beautiful parting song. "Okay, follow me!" Kevin cried, crawling into the rafters of the giant cathedral. Below them, the coronation ceremony had already begun.

Scarlet had arrived at Westminster Abbey in a stunning dress. As she looked around, she saw all her favorite villains watching her walk down the aisle. Scarlet waved at Tina Nelson and then gave a shout-out to the old organ player, Edna. Once she was in the front of the cathedral, surrounded by all the villains from Villain-Con in the audience, she couldn't help but smile. It was a dream come true.

Bob was still lugging the giant flower wreath on his head as he climbed off the roof. Suddenly, a bee emerged from one of the roses and started circling around his head. He tried to swat it away, but it didn't work. Stuart tried to smack it away but missed, hitting Bob in the goggles instead. The bug chased them off the rafters. Stuart and Bob ran...landing on the chandelier right above the altar.

"Do you, Scarlet Overkill, solemnly

promise...," the archbishop said as he held the crown in his hands.

The bee chased the Minions in circles, around and around the chandelier. Stuart and Bob kept running, trying to get away from it, but the more they ran, the more unsteady the chandelier became. The screw that held it to the roof came loose, and it started swinging back and forth. Kevin grabbed a support wire and climbed toward the chandelier. It looked like it might fall at any moment.

Far below, Scarlet smiled as the archbishop stepped forward with the crown. "I proclaim thee, with great reservation, the Queen of England!"

Kevin reached for his friends as the chandelier rocked back and forth. Hearing the commotion, Scarlet looked up in confusion. "Kevin?" she yelled.

Before Kevin could respond, the chandelier came loose from the ceiling. He managed to grab Stuart and Bob before it plummeted to the ground. It slammed down right on top of Scarlet.

"Scarlet! Scarlet, my queen!" Herb cried. "Someone help me!"

The Minions couldn't believe their eyes. They took hold of a nearby curtain and slid down it, into the massive crowd of villains. Some of the villains were helping Herb pull the chandelier off their master.

Bob was still holding the flower wreath. He handed it to Herb before disappearing into the crowd. Kevin and Stuart were searching for the exit. Maybe they didn't mean to hurt Scarlet, but they knew how this looked (not good).

They were almost at the door when they heard a crash behind them. Scarlet shot up toward the ceiling of the great cathedral. She had been protected from the chandelier by her dress—a new state-of-the-art villain suit that Herb had designed for her. She hovered there, staring down at the Minions, her face red with rage.

Kevin backed up, noticing how angry she was.

She pointed a finger at him. "He. Tried. To. Kill. Me," she said, barely able to get the words out.

"No!" Kevin shouted. It had been an accident: Scarlet was their master—they'd never want to see her get hurt.

But Scarlet wouldn't listen. "Villains…," she said, looking out at the crowd. "This is no longer a coronation. It's an execution. Get them!"

Chapter Eleven

The Minions took off running. They turned down one of the stone corridors in the abbey, trying to lose the angry crowd, but the villains followed close behind them. When they got to the end of the hall, they crashed through one of the stained glass windows. Seconds later, the villains came out of the cathedral, smashing through the brick wall.

As the Minions took off into the streets of London, one of the villains hurled a grenade at them. It landed just a few feet away, exploding in a ball of flames. The Minions darted into a telephone booth, trying to hide, but a villain in a terrifying hockey mask chased them out of it with a chainsaw. Another villain in a Soviet tank emerged from the ground, coming after Kevin, Stuart, and Bob with a huge ax.

"You're mine!" the Soviet villain cried.

"Stuart! Bob!" Kevin yelled when he got separated from his friends. Within seconds, he could no longer see them in the crowd. A villain with a long silver sword chased Kevin around and around a telephone pole, but Kevin managed to escape.

He kept glancing back, waiting to see Stuart or Bob emerge from the crowd, but they never did. He'd hoped they'd found some other escape route. They must've broken away from the villains when he wasn't looking. He kept running, his tiny legs sore from the effort, until he saw a pub up ahead. THE PIG'S SPLEEN read a sign out front. It seemed like a decent place to hide.

He ducked inside, watching as the crowd of

villains ran past. The pub was packed with people. A smaller group was huddled around a woman by the bar, laughing as she told them a joke.

"Why did the queen go to the dentist?" the woman asked. "To get her teeth crowned!"

Kevin recognized the woman's voice immediately. "La queena!" he cried, listening as she told another joke. He walked right up to her, offering a small smile. "Uh…bello…," he said.

The queen narrowed her blue eyes at him. "Oh. It's you," she said. "Everyone, this is one of the little fellows who stole the monarchy from me. And how's that working out for you?"

Kevin started telling the queen about the trouble he was in, but she stopped him. "Yes, yes. I saw what was happening on the telly." She pointed to the television set behind the bar. It showed the front of Westminster Abbey. A reporter was speaking into the camera, until Scarlet pushed him out of the way.

"Kevin, I know you're out there!" she yelled into the camera. "You think you've gotten away? Well, what do we have here?"

She reached down, pulling Stuart and Bob into the frame. They were both tied up. "Oh my goodness," Scarlet went on. "Which one shall I kill first? Little Bob? Stuart? Bob? Stuart? Hmmm? I will do it, Kevin, if you're not back here by dawn!"

She kicked the camera over, and the screen went to static.

"Oh dear...," the queen muttered.

But Kevin kept staring at the blank screen, thinking about his friends. He wasn't going to just stand there and let Scarlet kill them—not now, not ever.

"Buddies!" he yelled as he stormed out of the pub. "Lo peto Scarlet!"

"Les buddies!" he cried. Then he stomped off to find them.

Chapter Twelve

Stuart and Bob sat beside each other, tied to hundreds of sticks of dynamite. Scarlet had found every explosive in the city in her master plan to blow them up. The sun was rising, and there was still no sign of their buddy Kevin.

Herb knelt down and lit the fuse on the dynamite.

"This is it, boys. Things do NOT look good for you," Scarlet said. "Oh, and I'm keeping the bear." She held up Tim. "You won't need him where you're going...heaven." Bob called out for Tim.

Then Scarlet and Herb slunk away, disappearing behind a nearby building.

Meanwhile, a giant Kevin emerged from Scarlet's castle. All the villains who had been chasing him turned to flee. It didn't matter; he needed to hurry. The huge Kevin made his way through the city, hoping to save his buddies in time. But would he make it?

Stuart and Bob struggled against the rope. They tried to free their hands and legs, but it was no use. With every second, the fuse burned a little bit more, bringing them closer to their doom. Bob watched in panic as it got closer and closer....

Wham!

A giant boot slammed down on the fuse, snuffing it out.

"Bello, les buddies!" a giant Kevin cried out.

Kevin reached down, about to free his friends, when he heard something behind him. Scarlet had activated her dress. Turbines popped out of the back, allowing her to zip through the sky.

Weapons were activated on all sides of her jet pack—she had dozens to choose from.

"So that's your plan?" Scarlet shouted as she flew around him. "Make yourself a *bigger* target?"

With that, she hit her Lava-Lamp Gun, sending a molten stream right at Kevin. He ducked behind Big Ben just in time. The lava hit the bottom of the giant clock, tipping it over. Kevin reached down and grabbed it before it could hit the sidewalk.

Before Scarlet could fire at him again, Kevin grabbed Stuart and Bob and made a run for it. He darted down the streets of London, finally dropping his friends off before Scarlet could charge him again. She lunged off the side of a building and hit him full force.

Kevin fell, his head hitting the pavement. Scarlet hovered above him. "And so help me, I never want to see another one of your goofy, bug-eyed faces ever again!" she yelled.

But just then she turned, noticing a huge

crowd on the other side of the street. It was the Minions—not just Stuart and Bob, but all of them. They had traveled hundreds of miles, but they were here, in London, ready to fight. "You've got to be kidding me!" Scarlet said.

She aimed missiles at the tiny Minions. "Just for the record, you can thank Kevin for what I'm about to do to you!" The Minions huddled together, scared.

Just in time, Kevin smacked Scarlet away with his giant hand, sending her flying into a building. The Minions cheered for him! He was so happy to see his friends again. Kevin began kissing all his friends. Because of his size, he accidentally ended up with one Minion in his mouth. Stuart and Bob both ran over to hug their friends.

But Scarlet rose up again behind him, battered and furious. "Enough of this!" Scarlet growled. "This ends now!"

Scarlet's new dress activated into its final stage. It glowed and expanded, revealing a bomb right in the center of her chest. She aimed the explosive down at the Minions and fired.

Kevin could see the bomb dropping right over his friends. In seconds, they'd be blown apart. He couldn't bear the thought of them being hurt, so he took a step forward, leaned in…and swallowed it.

"Ha, ha, ha!" Scarlet laughed. "Have fun exploding!"

Scarlet grabbed Herb from below and flew up, wanting to get as far away from Kevin as possible. Kevin's mouth beeped, the bomb inside it ready to explode. But as soon as Scarlet took off, he grabbed her. She struggled, trying to get him off her, but it was no use. Within seconds, Scarlet, Herb, and a giant Kevin were all flying through the air.

The beeping sped up. The bomb was about to go off inside Kevin's stomach. "No, no, no, no, no!" Scarlet cried, still struggling to break free.

Boooooooooooom!

The bomb went off inside Kevin's stomach. Far below, on the ground, Stuart and Bob could barely watch the scene above. The sky was filled with smoke. Was their friend gone forever? Had the bomb killed him?

Bob wiped his eyes, trying not to cry. It took him a moment to notice the speck of yellow in the sky. From out of the cloud of smoke came a tiny Kevin, using his blue overalls as a parachute. "Looka!" Bob cried, showing the other Minions.

Not only had Kevin survived, he was back to his normal size. As he drifted down to the ground, all the Minions cheered. "Bello, buddies!" Kevin shouted.

They all squashed together in a group hug. Cops and palace guards swarmed the area, trying to keep order. The Minions had done it—they had saved all of London from Scarlet Overkill, the tyrant queen. But Scarlet's story wasn't over quite yet...

Scarlet and Herb hurtled through the sky in the malfunctioning rocket dress, flailing and screaming until...*WHAM!* They crashed in the middle of a snowy wasteland, skidding across the tundra and finally stopping at the entrance of a cave.

"What? Where are we?" Scarlet said as she brushed herself off.

She looked up and saw several angry-looking yetis standing over her. They were huge white and furry beasts, and they glared at her and growled. But Scarlet was not intimidated. In fact, they inspired her. Within hours, she became their queen and was holding the coronation ceremony she always wanted.

"This is my dream! My dream!" Scarlet said as a yeti placed a crown of fishbones on her head.

"My dreams are usually about me forgetting to wear pants. You have WAY cooler dreams than me," Herb replied.

Scarlet looked out at the many yetis, cheering

for her and throwing flowers. One of them was even crying. It was everything Scarlet had imagined.

"These wonderful, simple creatures NEED me. They LOVE me! I am the best queen EVER!"

Life works in mysterious ways. Scarlet and Herb finally had a kingdom to rule. It didn't have a castle, but it was air-conditioned. It was perfect. They were finally home.

Chapter Thirteen

"Ladies and gentlemen," Queen Elizabeth announced, addressing the giant crowd outside the palace. "We are here today to celebrate the Minions. The country owes you a great debt of gratitude."

Kevin, Stuart, and Bob stood beside her, brimming with pride. The audience was filled with London's residents, palace guards, and, of course, the giant tribe of Minions. "Bob," the queen went on, "you were a wise and noble king for all of eight hours. So for you, I offer this tiny crown for your teddy bear, Tim."

"Tri makasi! Tri makasi!" Bob cried, jumping up and down in excitement.

"Stuart," the queen continued, "for you I have this beautiful, super-duper incredible snow globe."

Stuart looked at the glass globe in his hand, trying hard to smile. He shook it and watched the plastic snow float in the water. It was kind of a strange present…but he guessed it would do.

"We're just messing with you!" The queen laughed. "Don't be mad at me—it was Kevin's idea." Then Kevin stepped forward with a beautiful red electric guitar for Stuart.

"Coolos!" Stuart said, smiling. He played an awesome solo for the crowd, who cheered for him. He really began to rock out there, and the crowd went wild!

"And finally, Kevin!" the queen said. "You are a hero of the highest order. For your bravery and valor, I am knighting you. From here on out, you are Sir Kevin. Well done."

"Kevin! Kevin! Kevin!" all the Minions

chanted. They carried their leader on their shoulders into the streets of London. Kevin had saved the day and won the love and respect of his tribe.

MINIONS ™

Don't miss these other great books!

Long Live King Bob!

Seek and Find

Poster Book

1000 Sticker Book

Fun Book

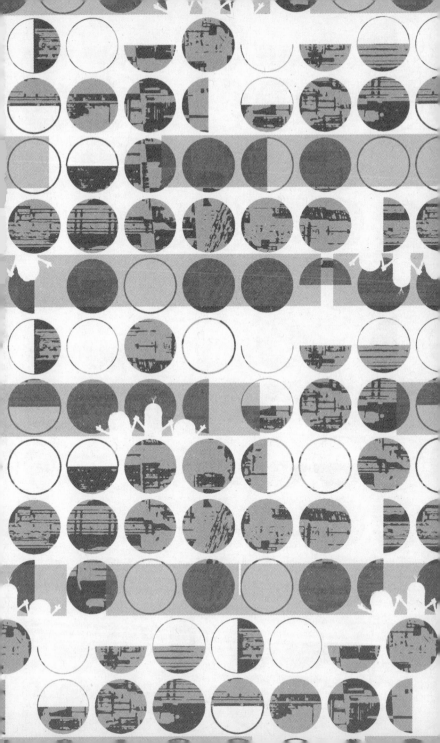

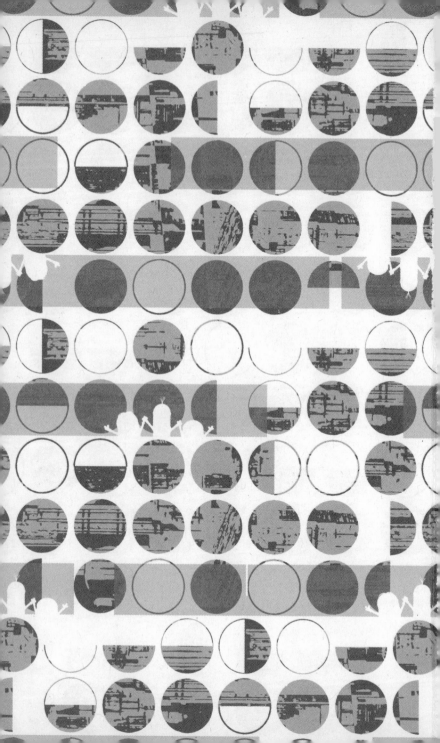